D1727184

THE Valley OF THE TROLLS

Illustrations: Rolf Lidberg
Original text: Robert Alsterblad
Translation: Berlitz AS
Publisher: Aune Forlag AS
Design: Aune Forlag AS/Jon Jonsson
Print: Tangen Grafiske Senter AS

Aune Forlag AS, Trondheim, Norway.
Art. No. 2589 Engelsk
ISBN: 82-90633-58-0

THE TROLLVALLEY

Rolf Lidberg

Join us on a journey through a year in the strange and colourful life of the trolls. See them on winter fishing trips and warm summer evenings. Meet the little troll girl, Fern, who scolds an old troll for shooting at elk, and get to know all the others who live in the Valley of the Trolls.

Christmas is over and the new year has just begun. It is a cold January night, and the sky is full of stars. The air is clear and bright. The pixie father is lying gazing at the stars with his youngest child. He has a dreamy look on his face.

"I wonder how the trolls are doing up in the Valley of the Trolls," says the pixie father. "Shall we wish ourselves there and have a look?" "Can we do that?" asks the little pixie. "Oh yes, pixies can do that," says the pixie father proudly.

When they reach the Valley of the Trolls, they meet some happy faces and some frowns. "Haven't you caught any fish?" one of the trolls asks another. The other troll, whose name is Sulky, is sitting and sulking. "There must be a spell on the fish. The holes are only a metre apart, but the fish will only bite at one of them," moans Sulky.

The more fish the first troll catches, the happier he becomes, while Sulky just gets in a worse and worse mood. "It's lucky that silly old troll will be leaving soon," thinks Sulky to himself. He knows that the other troll likes the countryside and always goes off walking in the spring in order to be the first to greet the spring flowers.

And of course the other troll is as lucky with the flowers as he is with the fish. The coltsfoot flowers by the side of the road are already in bloom, although it is only March. The troll raises his hat to welcome the flowers and the spring. On these spring walks he usually visits another troll who lives further up the Valley of the Trolls. There is something about that troll that makes him different from the other trolls and rather sad. Maybe a visitor will cheer him up?

Far up in the Valley of the Trolls he is sitting alone on a rock in the middle of a stream. He has been sitting there for several days with his feet trailing in the cold water, listening to the chirping of the birds. The birds are his best friends, and he understands their language.

He is bashful and shy, and prefers not to be with the other trolls. The reason is that one of his big toes is on the wrong side of his foot. When he has visitors he always keeps both feet under the water in order to hide his toes. "It doesn't matter where your big toe is," the other troll says to comfort him. A little bird chirps to them that Grandfather Troll is playing a bit further up the stream.

Grandfather Troll has been making a boat of bark and is now in the mood to play. He and the troll boy Bracken are on either side of the stream, blowing on the sail so that the boat moves backwards and forwards across the water. They put a new plant in the boat each time and guess what it is called. This is great fun and they could carry on for hours.

It is starting to get dark and they can hardly see the plants any more. Bracken says to his grandfather: "We can creep up to Troll Lake on tiptoe and spy on my sister so that she doesn't spend too much time kissing that boy from Troll Mountain. They are going on a boat trip, so you never know."

They sneak between the trees, and there is definitely romance in the air. At least on the part of the sister. She is kissing the boy. They spend the whole long, warm summer night in the boat, unaware that anyone is watching them. The sister hugs the boy tightly, but he is more interested in getting the fish to bite. “The troll boy from Troll Mountain looks OK,” whispers Bracken, “but I think my sister is clingy and annoying.” Grandfather Troll and Bracken doze off for a few hours, but wake up with a start at the sound of the farm girl blowing her birch-bark horn in the mountain pasture.

The horn can be heard throughout the Valley of the Trolls, and now lots of trolls are making their way up to the mountain pasture. Cows are milked, butter is made and bread is baked. Everyone is very busy with their tasks. The food stores have to be filled up before the winter. A couple of travelling farm musicians usually come and play, in return for food and a bed for a few nights. But the proudest of all must be Daisy the cow. Each day at milking time she gazes longingly across the Valley of the Trolls with a daisy in the corner of her mouth. “Maybe the bull will come soon …” she hums, but in cow language of course.

Summer has truly arrived, and Father Troll is sitting in the flowery meadow with his little troll daughter, Fern. He enjoys teaching his children all he knows about the flowers in the meadow. Fern shows him a beautiful bouquet she has picked. After that she tries to remember the name of each of the flowers. "You're a very clever girl," says Father Troll proudly, looking tenderly down at the little girl, before taking a well-deserved nap on the grass, tired after all the work he has done up on the mountain farm. "Now we'd better hurry home," he says when he wakes up again. "Tomorrow is the big annual elk-riding day. We mustn't miss that!"

Finally the day arrives for the biggest elk in the Valley of the Trolls to invite all the troll children for a ride. Mother Troll has packed their rucksacks full of food and drinks, and the troll children are arguing about who will be the first one to ride on the elk. The elk thinks this is the most fun day of the year, and Father Troll has to hold on to the elk's beard to stop him galloping off too fast.

The best place to sit on an elk is at the front by its horns, and the child that gets the most answers right to Father Troll's questions about flower names is allowed to sit there. Fern has obviously remembered most of the flower names from the day before, because there she is, proudly sitting by the elk's horns. But no-one can quite work out why the troll boy Bracken is also sitting there, when he is only interested in fishing.

Summer is over and it is time to go picking berries and mushrooms. Father Troll always wants to have a competition to see who can pick a whole basket first. Mother Troll has almost filled her basket when Father Troll shouts out, proud as a peacock: "My basket is full! I won, I won!" But the others are always suspicious, because Father Troll is good at cheating. "Look over there," says the troll boy, pointing at some very big mushrooms. Father Troll turns round so quickly that the basket almost falls off his arm. "Your basket seems very light," say the others suspiciously. Then they see that Father Troll has sneaked a thick layer of moss into the bottom of his basket. There is only a thin layer of mushrooms on top of the moss. What a rascal! The youngest troll boy is standing on the highest hilltop. He has caught sight of something down in the valley. Suddenly they hear a 'BANG!' echo between the mountainsides.

Isn't that Sulky, the troll who didn't catch any fish last winter? Now he's found his way into the woods to try his luck at hunting instead. "Don't you dare shoot our elks! They are our very best friends," scolds Fern, after quickly running down into the valley. "No … I wasn't shooting the elks, I was just shooting to warn them against other elk hunters." "What a dreadful story!" says Fern and continues scolding Sulky. In the end he is ashamed and promises hand on heart never to do it again. Later that day Fern has a brilliant idea which she tells Father Troll. He promises to do exactly as she said if any pixie children come knocking on his door before Christmas.

The first snow has come early and the winter stores are full. Sulky has gone back home and Fern is sure that he has already forgotten his promise not to shoot the elks. In the Valley of the Trolls two little pixies are going round selling comics and books for Christmas. They knock on the door of Mother and Father Troll's house. "I'll buy Asterix for my husband, because he looks just like him," laughs Mother Troll. "Buy Snoopy, and Winnie the Pooh," shout the troll children. "How babyish," says the oldest troll boy, "I want Donald Duck!" "Sorry, we haven't got that, but why not buy the new troll book and troll calendar that come out every year?" asks the youngest pixie politely. "That's a good idea," says Father Troll and buys them both. He collects all the troll books and enjoys reading about himself and all his relations. "We'll buy 'The Elk is the Trolls' Best Friend'," says Fern, "and we'll send it to Sulky before Christmas so that he remembers his promise."

JULNATT
TROLL-JUL

The November ice is already thick and strong. Father Troll takes two of the children out fishing through holes in the ice. As usual the fish only bite at one of the holes, so this time it is Father Troll's turn to feel what it is like not to catch any fish. Now he realises just how Sulky must have felt the previous spring.

The troll boys are whispering to one another, agreeing to tell Mother Troll that Father Troll caught the most fish. "That'll make him happy," they think. "It's best to be extra nice before Christmas."

At last Christmas is here, and the children are bursting with happiness and excitement. "The most important thing is not getting lots of presents," says Father Troll to his children, "but giving something of ourselves so that everyone can be happy and have a good life in the Valley of the Trolls." Santa Claus comes and gives each of them a present, and they all thank him politely. Father Troll says he does not want a present for himself. Instead he asks Santa Claus to give a present to Sulky. Maybe even Sulky will be happy then. "I already have the best Christmas present anyone could wish for – good troll children and a wonderful troll wife," says Father Troll proudly, giving Mother Troll a good hug.
"Do you want a hug too, daddy?" asks the youngest troll girl. "Strong or gentle?..." "Geeentle," mumbles Father Troll with pleasure, his eyes twinkling.

God Jul!
God Jul

This book belongs to

____

It was a present from

____

Rolf Lidberg

Few people can draw trolls better than Rolf Lidberg. His troll drawings have become collectors' items for tourists from all over the world. The secret of his success lies in his attitude towards nature. As a botanist and adventurer he presents the trolls in their true environment.